HOLD FOR RELEASE UNTIL THE END OF THE WORLD

C.V. HUNT

ATLATL

Atlatl Press
POB 293161
Dayton, Ohio 45429
www.atlatlpress.com

Other titles by C.V. Hunt

For Andy

1.

The meat was dry and twisted and the color of day-old jerky, clinging to the broken and sun-bleached bone. I leaned in closer and stared at what I presumed was the skinned and mangled carcass of a rabbit or possibly one of the neighborhood stray cats. It was hard to tell what kind of animal it was since it didn't have a head or fur. Whatever the creature had been in life it was now rotting directly on the disputable property line separating my yard from my cunt of a neighbor's yard. I'd first noticed the swarm of blow flies making a feast out of the small corpse while taking the trash out. At first I thought the insects were taking the opportunity to gorge on one of the numerous piles of dog shit scattered in my neighbor's yard. But the size of their meal and the bright white of the exposed bone caught my eye and told me this was something different. There was a moment of hopefulness as I recognized the small heap on the ground as an animal.

I cautiously approached it, making sure the neighbor wasn't lying in wait around the front of her house. She made it a habit to occasionally spring around the corner and verbally harass me with whatever delusion she'd cooked up since the last time she'd gone off her meds. Her latest obsession was to accuse me of sneaking over to her house in the middle of the night and rubbing my pussy on her door knob. Our last interaction left me speechless, slowly backing away from her toward my house as she threatened to decapitate me.

I tried to find anything recognizable about the lump of meat and bone. I thought maybe the neighbor's insistently yipping Chihuahua had finally expired and she was too out of her head to be bothered to do anything about it, or more likely, she wasn't physically able to bend over and pick it up. But what I was looking at didn't look like her dog and the hopefulness and giddiness building within me as I reveled in her misery and my triumph of one less grating sound among the cacophony of city noises came crashing down. It didn't look like anything.

It appeared as though one of the coyotes from the nature reserve behind our house had decided to abandon its meal conveniently on the imaginary line between two feuding neighbors. I didn't want to think the neighbor had done this out of spite. Because if she did it meant I was living next to a psychopath. I already thought she was a psychopath but something like this would confirm my flippant assessment of her since moving here six months previously.

The unmistakable slap of the neighbor's front screen door being thrown open and hitting the aluminum siding of her house broke my meditation over the dead animal. I retreated quickly across the narrow strip of grass, careful of any dog shit, as the neighbor liked to let her leashed dog cross the property line and defecate in my yard. I dodged down the driveway and ducked behind my car as the unmistakable jingle of the Chihuahua's leash and collar sounded shortly before a never ending series of maddening barks and snarls were hurled in my direction. I cursed under my breath. The dog had heard me.

I stood abruptly and hurried toward the back door of the house, which was technically a side door and completely in view of my neighbor. My neighbor made a sound I could only describe as a wounded wailing as I rounded the railing to climb the steps to the door.

The stairs to the door ascended toward the front of

the house, subjecting me to the view of my large, bowlegged neighbor in her ratty and stained T-shirt, sweatpants, and red ball cap yanking the leash of her tiny and furious dog as she glared at me, open-mouthed. For some reason she always reminded me of Michael Moore if you left Michael Moore out in a deluge of acid rain for ten years.

She yelled, "Keep yer pussy off my door, whore!"

I rushed inside and locked the door behind me. The yells of the neighbor and her dog were muffled but audible inside the house.

My roommate, Kebin, stood at the kitchen counter holding a cup of coffee, staring out the window at the backyard. He wore the same pajamas he'd been wearing the last five days and his greasy hair looked as though he'd just rolled out of bed but his alert eyes told me he'd been awake for hours.

Kebin said, "The shed door's open again." He took a sip of coffee without breaking his stare.

"What?" I said. I went to stand beside him and craned my head to look out the window.

On the left side of the yard was a garage acting as a barrier between us and our only neighbor . . . the crazy neighbor's backyard. To the right and behind the house was the nature preserve. We were the last house on our side of the street on the end of a dead end road in the city.

The garage had a screened in porch attached on the right side and, partially visible through the screens, stood the plastic kit shed we never used because it didn't have a lock and we didn't own more than a battery powered lawnmower Kebin had purchased online when we moved in and he kept the mower in the garage. I stared out the window and noted the shed door was indeed wide open.

The neighbor had stopped yelling but her dog continued to bark relentlessly.

"I'm not going back out there," I said and stood upright.

The overpowering smell of stale come, male sweat, and rotten onions wafted off Kebin. He sipped his coffee noisily, still staring out the window. I waited for him to offer to shut the door but he didn't respond.

"Are you going to take a shower today?" I said.

"Maybe tomorrow. I have work to do."

2.

Kebin found the house we were currently renting online six months ago through a barely literate post on the Kurtslist website. It was the same way he'd found me two years previously—a poor, forty-year-old, single female to be a surrogate mother and roommate. Kebin had wanted to share the rent of his overpriced and cramped apartment in the small town where he was attending a renowned liberal arts college that had gone defunct a couple of decades before but had reopened to offer overpriced and unaccredited courses to the rich yuppie/wannabe hippie kids of the alumni. Kebin's ad for a roommate stated he needed someone to cook his food, wash his laundry, pick up after him, and sometimes give him some words of encouragement since there were few female attendees at the college—most of the students being aware the school was unaccredited and therefore the education was useless in the real world. He had been unable to scam or coerce some unsuspecting girl into fucking him, becoming his girlfriend, moving in, and doing the aforementioned things he was too lazy to do himself.

So I had taken the position. Or become his roommate. However one wanted to look at it. I cooked and cleaned and paid half the rent and utilities in exchange for some peace and quiet and safety outside of Daxton.

Then Kebin 'graduated' after a couple of years and the full amount of his trust fund began to be distributed and he had an epiphany. He could spend *more* money from his trust fund each month if his rent was cheaper.

I mean . . . Daxton wasn't that bad, right? You could live there for half of what we paid to live in Green Falls. In my opinion, moving back to Daxton was about as appealing as being raped with a scorching hot curling iron, but I'd smiled and politely encouraged him to follow his dreams like a good surrogate mother.

And what were Kebin's dreams exactly? He wanted to become a great entrepreneur. He would invent and fund an app for locating and rating vaping supply stores across the world. He described it as Gelp for vape. Never mind actually using Gelp—a well-established crowd sourcing review app for every business—which already had located and rated most vaping supply stores in at least Daxton and Green Falls. By Gelp's recommendation The Smaüg Haus was the best place in Daxton to get your vaping supplies but Kebin said those reviews were tainted by non-serious vapers and people wrote parody reviews for Gelp and a dedicated app was the best solution for a serious vaper who needed quality supplies and friendly customer service.

In the end it was his money to do what he wanted with and it was my job to encourage him to follow his dreams. And I agreed to the move since my half of the rent would be cheaper and my drive to work would take half the time.

3.

Everything in Daxton was located on a dead end road. When you combined the dead end streets with the constant road construction it made it difficult to get anywhere. I wasn't sure how anyone ever got out of the city or how I managed to move back here. I just remember waking up one day after Kebin decided to move and I was in Daxton. Even my daily commute to my job was a blur.

My job was located on a dead end street. The building Financial Shaming, Inc. was located in was very luxurious. I and all the other employees knew the building was luxurious because even if one of us happened to be blind our boss, Donald P. Junkefeller, of the Junkefeller potato chip fortune, told us how luxurious the building was on a daily basis. Mr. Junkefeller, a scrawny and hunched man, would march back and forth in front of the employees in his expensive and ill-fitting Armani suit, waving his hands around to insinuate our surroundings, and shout, "Look at how luxurious this building is! I did an excellent job picking out this building, didn't I?! You all should be so lucky to work in such luxury!" To which all of the employees would nod like bobble heads and mutter agreement. It was part of the job. Because not only was Mr. Junkefeller the owner of Financial Shaming, Inc., he was a member.

On Monday I pulled into the parking lot of my job and spotted Sib lying prostrate on the hood of a Rolls-Royce. Sib's wheelchair sat empty a few feet from the car beside a well-groomed man who wore a leather tracksuit and had gold rings on every finger. The rings glinted in the sun as he crossed his arms and shouted something unintelligible at Sib. There were four small children in the car, barely discernible through the tinted glass of the closed windows, bouncing up and down in the leather seats.

I maneuvered my car past all the Porsches and Mercedes and the expensive cars of the clients and found a spot in the back lot for the employees. My car billowed a cloud of black smoke when I parked it and backfired something like a wet fart when I shut it off. I exited my piece of shit car held together with duct tape and a fond wish it would hold up until I was able to afford a car payment. I was forced to walk past the scene of Sib being humiliated on the hood of the Rolls-Royce by its owner to enter the building and knew better than to make eye contact with the client.

As I was passing the car I could hear the children within its closed interior laughing and carrying on.

Sib turned his head and spotted me. He said, "Oh, hey, Kurrie."

"Hey, Sib."

The man in the leather tracksuit bellowed, "Feel my wealth, scum! I want you to roll around on it!"

Sib twisted the upper half of his body and did his best to comply with the client's demands.

Sib spoke to me, "Brought my kids today, Kurrie. Mr. Junkefeller said he'd pay me an extra five dollars a day to shame my kids."

"That's right!" The client pointed angrily at the children in the car. "That's real calfskin leather! Smoother than your mama's cunt!"

The children in the car all repeatedly called 'yippee' through the closed windows as they continued to bounce up and down on the seats.

"Don't you think you should crack the windows," I

said to no one in particular.

"No!" the client yelled. "Those windows were specially ordered from a very expensive company in Nebraska! No one touches those windows! Who asked you, anyway?! I didn't ask for some chubby . . . old . . . saggy tits!"

"I'm sorry, sir," I said. "Please carry on."

I hurried toward the front door.

Sib called, "See ya later!"

The client called me degrading names and threatened to bend me over the hood of his expensive car and show me what kind of cock money could buy as I scanned my fob and entered Financial Shaming, Inc. I briefly wondered if I should ask Mr. Junkefeller for some of Sib's commission since I'd inadvertently gotten some of his shaming. But I knew Mr. Junkefeller would take the opportunity to tell me to go fuck myself and make condescending remarks to me the rest of the day even though he wasn't quite smart enough to know how condescension worked.

I quickly made my way to my cubicle. I passed one man laughing at a younger female coworker, known only as 'the crier', as she wore a nice fur coat and sobbed openly and red-facedly. There was a woman in a pant suit shoving her tax returns in the face of an elderly gentleman and repeatedly barking, "How much do *you* make?" The cubicle next to mine housed a caged opossum and a teenager—the teenager most likely belonging to one of the adult clients—and the teenager repeatedly poked the opossum with a stick and cackled uncontrollably.

My cubicle contained one chair with a strange stain on the seat and a framed piece of paper with 'Fuck you your pour peice of shit! – Donald P. Junkefeller' poorly handwritten and hung on the back wall for anyone to see who walked past. I took my seat and waited for a client.

4.

I drove down the dead end street where I lived and could feel the terrible anxiety and panic building the closer I got to the house. Every time I drove down this road I dreaded the thought of arriving at the house and finding the psychotic neighbor standing in her yard with her dog, waiting to take her verbal shots at me, free of charge. It was one thing to get paid by rich clients to get yelled at and be degraded but having someone who made even less money than I did shouting things at me for free was completely different.

Fortunately, the neighbor was nowhere to be seen. But there was a small child standing on the sidewalk at the house across the street, alone and eating an ice cream bar.

My car thankfully didn't backfire when I parked it in the drive beside the house, which would have been the signal for my neighbor to know I was home and outside for at least a minute as I checked the mail. Thankfully I was always able to park in our driveway, close to the side door, since Kebin didn't own a car. Somehow he'd always managed to live within walking distance of everything he needed or was able to con someone into chaperoning him wherever he needed to go. Another key point for his decision to move to this house was the bus stop two blocks down the road. Never mind the stop was nearly defunct and a bus was only scheduled to stop twice a day, once in the morning and once in the evening, and it didn't run at all on the weekends.

As I walked toward the front of the house to check the mail the child across the street spotted someone down the street I wasn't able to see from my location.

The child raised his ice cream and shouted, "Jom! Jom! Jom! The creep in the van gave me ice cream again! Jom! Jom!" He took a bite of the ice cream and raised it again. "Hey, Jom! Ice cream! The creep gave me ice cream! The creep in the van!"

I found a jury duty notice in the mailbox and couldn't remember registering to vote since I'd moved back to

Daxton. I retreated to the side of the house and before turning to climb the steps I noticed the door to the shed was open again, or Kebin hadn't bothered to close it from before. I sighed and resigned to closing it myself since the neighbor wasn't outside at the moment.

The grass in the backyard was overgrown and I wondered when the last time Kebin had mowed it was. I knew even if I mentioned it to him I would still get stuck doing it the coming weekend. I trudged through the grass and back to the shed. Inside the shed I found a large pile of old clothes and newspapers and ripped up cardboard boxes on the floor. The structure didn't have any electricity and someone had managed to tie a black garbage bag around the shitty plastic skylight that normally allowed a sickly and scant amount of sunlight to filter through. There was also an indentation in the scattered junk on the floor. It appeared as though someone might have been using the rubbish as a makeshift bed and the trash was smashed and packed down and I knew if the shed would ever need to be cleaned the garbage would need to be shoveled out.

As I closed the doors an awful stench wafted out and blew in my face. The shed smelled of death and dirt and something I couldn't quite place but it made me gag.

I walked back to the house. When I reached the top of the steps I spotted the kid on the other side of the street again. He had either finished or abandoned his ice cream and now had each of his hands on the extended handle of a piece of wheeled luggage and was pulling them down the sidewalk toward an unmarked white van.

I opened the door to the house and the sound of disjointed techno music blasted out. I stepped into the kitchen. There seemed to be a lot of ruckus coming from the living room. I dropped the jury duty notice in the trash and walked into the living room. Kebin was flailing about in the center of the room wearing only a pair of sequined red shorts that were extremely snug.

"You're home!" he shouted over the din.

"Yeah," I said, "I think we have a homeless person living in our shed."

Kebin continued to jump around and swing his arms in an unusual manner. "What?!"

I yelled, "There's a homeless person living in our shed!"

"Oh! Did you talk to him?"

He thrust his chest out, swung his arms straight down and behind him, and did what I could only construe as jazz hands before jogging in place.

"Can we turn the music down?! So we don't have to shout?!"

"Oh! Sure!" Kebin danced over to the stereo and lowered the volume to a whisper. "I had the sudden urge to dance!" He shouted even though there wasn't a need to anymore. "I thought it might get the creative juices flow-ing! How was my dancing?!"

"It was very good."

He spoke at a normal volume. "Did you talk to the tenant?"

"Tenant?"

"Yeah. I'm renting the shed out. I found this site online where you can rent rooms or your whole house to people who are traveling. It's called Skybnb. I walked back there to close the shed door this morning and couldn't help but think how much of a waste of space it was. It seemed like the perfect opportunity to make some money so I did a little research."

"Why didn't you rent out the third bedroom upstairs? Neither one of us goes up there."

"I don't want strangers staying in the house. They might find out about my app and steal the idea. Besides, they're not on the lease and I don't want to get in trouble with the landlord."

"But isn't renting the shed still technically considered subletting?"

"No. It's not part of the house. It's just a plastic shed."

I didn't have the energy to argue with him.

"Oh," he said, "and I didn't have to buy a bed. I went on a walk and collected some of the random stuff people threw along the bike path in the nature preserve and made a bed."

"Okay."

"Did you talk to the guy? He's staying for a few weeks. He's on vacation."

"To Daxton?"

Kebin nodded. "I told him he could use our bathroom but he declined."

"I didn't see him."

"Too bad. He's a pretty cool guy. Do you want to watch me dance and give me words of encouragement?"

"Can I eat some dinner first?"

Kebin's enthusiasm disappeared. His shoulders slumped and he stared at the floor dejectedly. "I guess."

5.

I woke up to my phone making a noise like a hysterical old woman wailing instead of the usual sound of
my alarm. I grabbed the phone and tried to clear the
sleep from my eyes and brain as I read the alert flashing
on the screen: Daxton is on fire!!!!!

My phone was old and the touchscreen had never
worked correctly. I tapped the screen and tried to shut the
alert off but my phone continued to wail. I forcefully hit
the touchscreen button repeatedly until the phone decided
it was time to be silent. I groaned and noticed the time
was five minutes before my alarm was scheduled to sound.
I shut off the alarm and checked the news on my phone

while my bladder ached to be relieved. A wildfire had started across the river, near downtown. I wasn't sure how a wildfire was possible in an urban area.

I left my bed and looked out my window. My room was at the rear of the house and the window looked out over the backyard. I didn't see anything indicating a wildfire. My sense of direction had always been poor and I wasn't even sure if I was facing downtown. The sky was the same sickly yellow it was most mornings but most notable was the figure lurking across the far end of the backyard.

A person dressed in a long black coat dragging on the ground was slowly walking along the tree line, holding a black umbrella close to their head. The umbrella blocked their face and it was difficult to discern much about them. It appeared as though they'd emerged from the overgrown path leading into the nature preserve. I had briefly debated taking the path once when we'd moved in but I was certain the foliage covering it was poison ivy and decided against it. The person clad in black crept into the shed and pulled the door shut. I figured it was safe to assume he was the tenant.

I went about my daily routine. Kebin's room, next to my own, and at the front of the house, was quiet as I got ready for work. I stared out the kitchen window as the coffee pot did its job. I was hoping to catch another glimpse of our tenant but he never reemerged from the shed. The sky continued to stay the same shade of yellow it had been when I woke up and there seemed to be an exuberant amount of tiny black bugs flying about lackadaisically. It wasn't until I exited the house that I saw the large, thick black cloud of smoke in the distance. And the small black bugs weren't bugs but raining pieces of ash.

6.

The grocery store parking lot was a nightmare of honking horns and pedestrians who either looked lost or angry as they pushed their bounty to their cars or, in some cases, toward the bus stop ten feet from the door. The horde of people was mainly comprised of angry tricenarians dressed like teenagers from fifteen fashion seasons past or quadragenarians rode so hard on prescription pill abuse, alcoholism, and sheer depression they looked either homeless or thirty years older than what they actually were.

I maneuvered my car around a homeless man standing beside an empty parking spot. He held a cardboard sign with 'will incert things in my anus for fuud' printed in very straight and neat script which indicated any money given to him might actually be used for something useful and he wasn't experiencing withdrawals from whatever drug of choice most people in Daxton chose to numb themselves with. I avoided making eye contact with the man with the sign as I exited my car and made my way quickly and cautiously across the parking lot.

I dodged out of the path of a few cars with raging drivers who honked at me and screamed for me to get out of the fucking way. But escaping the rampaging paths of the pedestrians with carts was always more difficult.

One woman who looked like she'd lifted herself off a barroom floor before coming to the store braced the handle of her cart, glared at me, and came rushing at me. I jumped to the right and she corrected her cart to keep me in target. I dove to the left, fell, and did a half summersault before righting myself. She missed me and plowed the cart full force into the back of someone's car.

Her head snapped in my direction and she spat, "Crazy bitch! Didn't you see me?! Get the fuck out of the way!"

"Sorry!" I said and took off in a half jog toward the store.

A woman who looked like a rabid soccer mom was next. Her bobbed and stacked haircut was accentuated with multiple unnatural chunky streaks, each streak a different shade of natural hair color, none of which were her own. She braced the handle of her shopping cart like a linebacker and came barreling at me. I rolled across the hood of someone's car at the last second to avoid being hospitalized while the woman screamed, "What the fuck is the matter with you?!"

I managed to make it to the door without being trampled by one of the many angry shoppers as they made their way to their vehicles. I was almost hit by a car as I played a *Frogger*-like game at the last stretch of asphalt separating the parking lot from the semi safety of the store's sidewalk.

As I reached the doors a man's voice rose out of the chaos.

"Miss! Miss! Miss!"

At first I ignored him. I couldn't imagine someone using the endearing term to refer to me. Miss was what one would call a pretty and young girl. Not an overweight, forty-year-old woman. But the man's insistence increased as I was about to cross over the threshold and into the store.

"Miss! Miss! Miss!"

I turned and spotted a rail-thin man approaching from the direction of the bus stop. He wore a baseball cap, an oversized baseball jersey, and satiny basketball shorts. The sensors for the doors I was standing in front of triggered and opened the glass doors and I managed to move out of the way just as another shopper hurled out of the store with their cart and screamed obscenities at me.

The man stopped five feet from me and said, "Miss, do you happen to have a cigarette?"

"I'm sorry," I said. "I don't smoke."

His face twisted into fury. "Well, you're a fucking bitch."

"Okay," I said and entered the store.

The entryway to the store where the shopping carts were normally stored was empty except for a handful of ransacked racks that normally housed some local free papers, three kiddie vending machines someone had shattered the glass to and emptied, and a few broken carts. I picked the cart with the most amount of wheels—which totaled three since the front right one was missing—and struggled with it as I entered the store.

The din of the parking lot could not compare to the cacophony of noise inside the store. The first thing I was confronted with were the checkout lanes which was a mob of cashiers and customers bitching at each other, mingled with the sound of several wailing children. I tried to make quick work of passing the area but the absence of the fourth wheel on my cart made moving quickly impossible. I was forced to pull back on the handle on the left side to keep the front end of the cart from dragging on the floor.

At the end of the row of checkout lanes a man wearing either a police uniform or a security uniform resembling a local police officer's uniform was beating an elderly woman relentlessly with a night stick while she lay on the floor surrounded by broken and smashed produce, shielding herself with her arm.

I passed the beating and barreled into the produce section. I threw some overpriced and wilted lettuce in the cart along with some slightly moldy tomatoes. I gave up on the produce section once a man decided to repeatedly ram his cart into mine and call me a cunt because my cart happened to be sitting in the exact spot he wanted to stand so he could stare at the carrots.

Next was the bread. Two men were fist fighting in the bread aisle. There was no bread on the shelves but several loaves were on the floor, smashed and trampled and flecked with blood as the two men relentlessly pounded each other's faces. The fate of the bread was becoming more compromised by the handful of other shoppers tromping down the aisle and picking through the wreckage. I became one of those people and snagged up a loaf of unmarred bread without inspecting it and later found out it was stale and moldy potato bread.

I emerged from the aisle and found myself in the meat and deli section. There was a line of people shouting at the deli employees. And I spotted a person clad in all black with a black umbrella, which hid their face, standing by the greenish cuts of beef, motionless. I pushed and pulled my cart in their direction. I grabbed handfuls of random half-spoiled meat and tossed them in the cart, trying to get a look at the figure's face. I was certain it was the same person living in the shed even though I hadn't gotten a look at their face then. But the figure managed to turn and disappear into the crowd, keeping their face hidden from me the whole time. Someone rammed my cart with their own and I knew it was time for me to move on.

We needed toilet paper but I wasn't able to find it since the store had taken to rearranging the location where everything was stocked on a weekly basis. I did happen to find some napkins, which would have to do, after I abandoned my cart for a few brief seconds and squeezed by a group of three shoppers who'd decided to stop in the middle of the aisle, blocking any other shoppers from passing, to have a conversation. They'd become engrossed in their own conversation and grown oblivious to their surroundings. I'd shouted 'excuse me' five times before sidling by them. I was certain I would be able to pass them without any incident because they seemed unaware of me but one of the people from the group glared at me on the return pass while I held the napkins above my head and tried not to disturb them.

I grabbed a handful of random canned goods from the

shelves I passed, struggling with the integrity of my cart and fending off other aggressive shoppers, and made my way toward the end of the store.

A small child sat on top of a shelf and threw cans of tuna at the shoppers, laughing hysterically if he happened to hit one in the head. He didn't manage to hit me but he did deposit several cans in my cart. I passed a large man choking a woman as she hit him in the head with a package of diapers and an infant wailed wildly in an abandoned cart. Once I made it to the end of the store I knew I was at the worst part before the checkout lanes . . . the pharmacy.

A man was shouting at someone cowering behind the counter in the pharmacy pickup area while waving around a lit cigarette. Someone with a backpack and a ski mask hopped the counter and started shoving random bottles of pills into their bag. The other pharmacy technicians pelted the masked person with random bottles and objects within their reach.

Shoppers in the raided aisles of the over-the-counter medicine and aids and bandages shouted random questions at the workers in the pharmacy.

A woman shouted, "I have herpes! Will calamine make my vag stop itching?!"

An old man shouted, "Can I swallow suppositories?! I'm not an ass pirate and I'm not sticking anything in my ass!"

Another person. "I have a rash!"

And another. "My kid has a fever of a hundred and seven!"

The masked man raiding the pharmacy pulled a firearm from the band of his pants and waved it around. The technicians all hit the floor. The shoppers continued their endless questioning as I hurriedly passed the havoc.

"What's causing this rash?!"

"Where's the lube?! My pussy is really dry!"

"Oh, god! I just shit myself!"

I made it to the checkout lanes before I heard the gunshots and screams. I held onto the cart handle and put my head down, anticipating what would happen next. Half of the people in the store rushed toward the doors in a panic, knocking over the display cases for energy drinks and trampling small children and the elderly in the process. Most of the shoppers on line to check out abandoned their carts and joined the mob.

"Amateurs," I muttered to myself.

The group of people milling about on the observation deck above the front doors cheered. A woman in an evening gown, draped in expensive furs, raised her champagne glass and laughed loudly as she watched the mass of people below her. A man in a tuxedo beside her raised a paper ticket and was shouting he had the correct time stamp as a few other men around him crumbled their tickets and puffed on their cigars. A servant wearing a tux with tails approached the luxurious couple with a covered silver platter. He lifted the lid and exhibited banded stacks of cash and displayed the platter to the ticket-holding man with a flourish. The woman picked up one of the stacks of cash and rubbed it against her face with an expression of pure ecstasy and I wasn't able to hear her over the din but I imagined she was moaning as she did so.

When the dust had cleared and the people who had rushed the doors were gone the employees hidden under the registers slowly lifted their heads, checking to make sure it was all clear. They didn't bother to make sure the shooter was gone. The shooter most definitely had disappeared into the mob anyway. The employees were only checking to make sure the stampede was over.

I wasn't the only person who'd taken their chance and stayed. One dirty and disheveled woman had continued to haggle with the cashier about the price of a can of corn as if she were at a flea market instead of a grocery store.

The dirty woman berated her cashier. "I don't care if it scans seventy-five cents! I'm only paying fifty cents for that! It has a small tear in the label!"

A female cashier who appeared exhausted and wore smudged blue eyeliner and had slicked back her hair into a high ponytail emerged from under the register. "Ma'am, you can't barter for your groceries."

"These prices are ridiculous! I demand to see the manager!"

"You have demanded to see the manager after every item I've scanned up to this point because you don't want to pay the stickered price. And I will give you the same answer I gave you when I scanned the previous"—the cashier turned to look at her screen—"thirty-seven items. Our manager quit over a week ago. If you have an issue you need to call our corporate headquarters."

"Fine!"

The cashier placed the can of corn in the accumulating bags and grabbed the next item, which appeared to be the second to last item in the woman's order. She scanned the item and the dirty woman went on another tirade of refusing to pay the price the computer had displayed and demanding to see the manager.

I left my cart and began clearing the carts out of one lane with a waiting cashier.

When the other woman was told her total she began to haggle that price also. And then they moved on to her twenty expired coupons.

Once I had all but one cart out of the way I swept the remaining items of someone's abandoned purchase into the cart with my arm before roughly shoving the cart out of the lane.

The employee stationed there was a pimple-faced kid. Or maybe he was covered in meth sores. It was hard to tell anymore. He watched me with a scowl as I fought to push my three-wheeled cart through the rubble.

I unloaded my cart onto the conveyer and told the cashier to start a new sale as multiple sirens grew louder outside. The customer in the other lane asked if she could write a check and the group of people on the observation deck broke out into a fit of hysterics.

7.

The day was warm and since I didn't have air conditioning in my car I rolled down all the windows on my way to work. The wildfire was still raging and the ash swirled in and out of my car as I drove down the highway. By the time I reached my exit I felt gritty and in need of another shower.

I turned on my road and spotted a new creep at the daycare center today. There were three large electrical transformer boxes situated along the edge of the property of the daycare. A sidewalk separated the boxes from the playground fence. A sleazy looking man in a fedora and trench coat sat on one of the boxes, staring longingly at the play yard as the children lined the fence and worked their tiny fingers through the chain links.

As I drove by I could hear the children chanting out of unison, "Pick me! Pick me! Pick me!"

Nothing appeared out of the ordinary once I arrived at work. I went through my regular rigmarole and passed a man holding a card up to one of the employees' faces as he explained to them the card was an AAirpass and he'd paid three million dollars for it so he could fly unlimited first class for the rest of his life and there were only sixty-five other members in the world.

In Sib's cubicle a woman smoked a Sobranie cigarette and fanned herself with some papers as he sat in his wheelchair watching her expectantly. I assumed the papers were car titles because she kept repeating, "I own five Lamborghinis." And then she would blow smoke in Sib's face.

Mr. Junkefeller charged into my cubicle. His nose was red and there were dark circles under his eyes. He held a martini glass and shouted in a nasally voice, "I'm sick! I don't feel good! I have all the money in the world and I should be invincible!"

"I'm sorry you don't feel well, sir," I said.

"Why are you covered in soot?! You look like a chimney sweep! You look extra poor covered in soot! Like an orphan from *Mary Poppins*!"

"The wildfire, sir. I don't have air conditioning in my c—"

"I don't give a good god damn about your poor people problems!"

"I'm sorry, sir."

"Yeah?! You better be sorry!" He slurped noisily from his martini glass. "I only drink vodka that's been poured over the breasts of the finest German models! Do you have any idea how much a bottle of this vodka costs?!"

"No, sir."

"Two hundred and sixty dollars, you pathetic poor piece of shit! More than you'll ever be able to afford! I'm drinking the finest vodka in the world to sterilize my insides! Because I'm sick!"

"That's a lot of money."

"Pocket change!" he barked. He threw back the last of the drink and made a satisfied sound. "I wish I wasn't sick so I could taste those German nipples!"

A client from another cubicle shouted, "I hate foreigners! We should deport them all! Fuck the Germans!"

Mr. Junkefeller shouted at no one in particular. "Who would I ridicule if it weren't for foreigners and the poor?! We should deport you!" He threw his martini glass against the wall and it shattered into a million pieces.

I covered my head with my arms and small pinpricks of pain emanated from the cuts as the glass sliced my skin.

Another client shouted, "Being racist is fun!"

Mr. Junkefeller shouted at me, "I'm sick! I don't feel good! Clean up that glass with your bare hands before I fire you! And when you're done I want you to polish all of my Rolexes! And you better start crying about your financial plight before I get really mad and pay a bum to beat your ass!"

8.

The neighbor was standing on the sidewalk in the middle of our driveway. She was facing our house and her dog had stretched its leash into our yard and was hunched into the universal crouch of a shitting dog. I stopped the car at the end of the driveway. She continued to stare at the house and was either oblivious I was waiting for her to get out of our driveway or was ignoring me on purpose. Her dog finished shitting and joined her before barking at my car. The neighbor slowly broke from her possibly drug-induced haze and turned toward me. She took her sweet time waddling into her own yard, yanking on the barking dog's leash, scowl-

ing at me the entire time.

I pulled into the driveway cautiously, terrified she might lose control of the dog and it charge under the tire of my car. I noticed a small package sitting on the front step and realized the neighbor had been staring at it while her dog shat. My car let loose a series of backfires before it died. The neighbor let loose a string of profanities that ended with her threatening to beat my ass before she retreated into her house. I waited for the slap of her screen door before I exited my car.

My plan was to grab the box on the step and the mail before the neighbor decided she wasn't done shouting at me but I spotted something in the grass near the mailbox. I wasn't sure what it was at first but as I got closer it was apparent it was another mangled animal. This one was fresher than the previous one. I didn't see any bones. Only a pile of bloody meat topped with what looked like scattered human teeth. A few blow flies buzzed around the meat angrily.

I hurriedly grabbed a letter out of the mail box and noticed it was from the City of Daxton. I grabbed the box and read the shipping label. The package was for 'Grim, The Unpleasant' but at our address. I knew it wasn't for me because I was too poor to order anything. I assumed it was some new alias and scheme Kebin was cooking up.

When I turned to walk back to the side door I almost

ran into the figure staying in our shed. He stood on the narrow section of sidewalk leading around the house, clad in a black robe, holding the black umbrella down low enough I was only able to make out the bottom of his pale face. He extended a pale hand with black pointy nails in my direction without a word.

I stared at him, dumbfounded, before I realized he was asking for the package.

I said, "Are you Grim, The Unpleasant?"

He nodded. I reluctantly handed him the package. He turned abruptly and retreated around the corner of the house in a flourish of billowing robes. I hurried after him but by the time I made it to the backyard he had disappeared. The shed door stood open and the structure was empty.

9.

City of Daxton
123 Main Street
Daxton, 'Muricahio 01313

Insufficient Junk Courtesy Letter

Dear Resident,

The City of Daxton (the "City") is sending you this *Insufficient Junk Courtesy Letter* due to the increasing problems with insufficient junk in lots throughout the City and the constant complaints from residents complying with

The City's Code of Ordinances. Please note Section 78-91 of The City's Code of Ordinances prohibits, among other things, an insufficient amount of junk to be viewable on every property from the sidewalk and or street. You are required as a resident of The City to maintain an adequate amount of debris and rubbish on your lawn at all times. More specifically, Section 78-91 states as follows:

It shall be unlawful for any owner of a lot, parcel, or tract of land within the city to permit the said property to remain unmolested by at least three of the following items: old tires, spare car parts, children's toys, an up-turned swing set (children's or adult's) or hammock, an unkempt wood pile, a baby's stroller or playpen, ten pounds of dog feces, an incapacitated car, random articles of clothing, a scattered thirty-gallon bag of garbage (must include at least five soiled infant diapers), random rusted metal, a unlicensed car trailer, an unrepairable and non-functioning motorcycle/ATV/boat, overgrown grass of at least fifteen inches in height, animal carcasses, broken patio furniture, a half constructed/damaged and abandoned luxury item such as a gazebo or pool.

City of Daxton's Code of Ordinances, § 78-91. Accordingly, please obey the above Code provisions and let your property fall to waste in compliance with those provisions as failure to do so will result in your property receiving a violation.

Should you have any questions or concerns about this notice or the ordinance, please feel free to go fuck yourself.

Sincerely,
City of Daxton

10.

My birthday was fast approaching. I remembered to check my driver's license expiration date and was filled with dread when I realized it would need to be renewed. I decided to take an extended lunch the next day and make the trip to the Bureau of Motor Vehicles and get it out of the way before I forgot.

My client before lunch tried to run our session long by bringing her chauffeur with her and forcing me to ask the chauffeur for a ride while he explained to me in a condescending manner I was too poor for him to drive me around. The client laughed and told me I should be striving to reach the chauffeur's level of poorness which she deemed more acceptable than my own because he was employed to serve a purpose for a rich person. I refrained from informing her the act of her paying me for her to be delighted in my humiliation was just what she was telling me to strive for. She told us to repeat our dialogue and laughed at me each time the chauffeur refused me a ride but after the sixth time I had to excuse myself for lunch.

I got lost three times, each time on a dead end road, was forced to pass the exit I needed because of construction, took the next exit which led into a junkyard, and eventually managed to find a random road within the mountains of rubble—some of which were on fire and filling the already ashen sky with more black smoke—without puncturing a tire. I drove up and down the road the Bureau was supposed to be located on looking for the address but there was no building with the number I'd found online and it wasn't until my eighth pass down the road that I spotted the place hidden behind a bank that appeared to have gone out of business. The Bureau wasn't actually located on the road of the address listed online but on a road that intersected with it.

The parking lot was full of cars. Gaggles of small children and slow moving elderly migrated in and out of the building.

I was forced to stop and wait as a red car parked

sideways and took up the driveway just as I pulled into the lot. I could make out a teenage girl behind the wheel. I assumed she was there for her driving test because an elderly man wearing a helmet sat in the passenger seat and kept pointing to things while the girl wrung her hands around the steering wheel. She pulled the gear shift on the column of the wheel and backed the red car into a parked van, pulled forward a few feet, and gunned the gas to hit the van again, harder. The instructor in the passenger seat nodded agreeably and mimed some directions. I waited patiently as the girl unbuckled her seatbelt, jumped out of the car, keyed the word 'cunt' across the side of the van, jumped back in the car, and squealed her tires as she sped through the parking lot. She almost hit two small children fist fighting behind one car and clipped an old lady's walker as she was taking too long to cross the drive before pulling out on the road and blowing through the red light at the intersection. I was certain the girl would be getting her license today.

I found one empty parking spot left. The car parked on the driver's side had pulled in at a bizarre angle with their front driver's tire touching the parking spot line on the driver's side and the back passenger tire hanging a foot over the line into the empty spot. The enormous truck thing parked on the passenger side of the empty spot was so large its entire driver's side hung a foot over into the empty spot. I carefully positioned my car, got a good running start, and floored the accelerator. The front corner of my car hit the crooked car with enough force to shove the other car forward, sending it over the cement parking stop. My passenger side mirror snapped off as the entire passenger side protested and scraped down the truck's side. I had to gun my car a few more times before I was completely in the spot. The car that had jumped the parking stop was now in such a position I was forced to exit my car by rolling down the window and climbing out and over the trunk of the other car.

Other cars raced through the lot, trying to find a space to park. Some of them decided to abandon their cars in the middle of the drive and entered the building. I dodged around feral children and slow-moving elderly, being vigilant of the disgruntled drivers, until I reached the building.

Inside the Bureau of Motor Vehicles was even more chaotic. I second-guessed myself and had to double check and make sure I had entered the correct building. About two dozen children were running and doing flips and screaming and crying and singing in the aisles of the crammed waiting room, which had rows of seats set up like an airport terminal area. The seats were almost filled to capacity. Most of the people seated were elderly or handicapped and, combined with the wild and unruly children, I felt as though I'd stepped into some type of daycare for all three categories. There was an enormous counter with ten clerks, each of them busy helping a person. One clerk at the end of the counter was administering a tattoo to the side of an elderly woman's neck as she wept openly. There was an overhead screen with the red number seventy-two illuminated on it and a stand in the center of all the chaos holding a number paper ticket dispenser.

I approached the ticket dispenser and found a number of spent tickets littering the floor and the actual ticket dispensing contraption was empty. Some of the tickets were print side up: Five hundred thirty-one, three thousand nine hundred twenty-seven, and seven hundred seventy-seven. I spotted one with one hundred thirty-three printed on it. As I bent to retrieve the ticket two children ran toward me and tried to kick the tiny paper away from my hand while laughing. I managed to snag the number before the children began scooping up handfuls of the numbered tickets from the floor and throwing them in the air like confetti, whooping cheerfully.

I found an empty seat beside a middle-aged woman who reeked of diaper rash cream and was involved heavily in playing Disgruntled Fish on her oversized phone. I closed my eyes and tried to block out the scene around me when I was startled by the sound of a bullhorn and someone shouting the number seventy-three.

It took two hours for my number to be called and I knew Mr. Junkefeller was going to be pissed I'd been gone so long and I would have to endure a double dose of humiliation from him when I returned to work. I briefly debated calling work after the first hour to inform them I would be later than I'd anticipated getting back but it would've only doubled my humiliation by having Mr. Junkefeller yell at me over the phone for half an hour *plus* whatever he would have in store for me once I returned. Also, I didn't want to be one of those assholes who think they're so fucking important they have to make phone calls and conduct their business or private affairs in public. I'd gotten my fill of that while waiting from an elderly gentleman who'd taken up a seat behind me and decided to fill his wait time by giving a play-by-play account of the debacle happening around us to whom I could only imagine was his wife. The man also spent at least thirty minutes arguing with the other person and accusing them of fucking someone else because they didn't pick up until the fifth ring and they usually answered it in less than two.

When the bullhorn sounded and my number was called I was helped by a short and stocky woman with a black eye. It was hard not to stare at her black eye and wonder how she got it.

The woman said, "What ya need?" in a clipped tone.

I pulled my driver's license from my pocket and laid it on the counter. "I need to renew my license."

The woman sighed heavily, slapped her hand over the license, and slid it off the counter. She laid the card on the keyboard of her computer and began typing angrily by stabbing the keys with her bony and calloused fingertips.

She said, "All the information the same?"

"My address changed."

She stopped typing and stared daggers at me. An awkward moment passed between us when a child ran behind me and punched me in the back of the thigh. I fell into the counter and the child ran off. A seated woman yelled at someone named Petey and told them to stop punching people or she was going to punch them. The woman behind the counter was growing more frustrated.

"Well," the woman barked, "what is it?"

I rubbed the back of my thigh. "What's what?"

"You're ad . . . dress." She dragged the word out as if she were speaking to someone simple.

I told her the address of the house and her fingers flew across the keyboard.

"Are ya sure this is your correct weight?" she said.

"What does it say?"

"A hundred and forty."

"Sounds about right."

I wasn't completely sure because I didn't care what I

weighed. There didn't seem to be any point in maintaining a shapely figure when literally no man or woman had shown any sexual interest in me in the last ten years. I didn't want to know what my weight was because it would only make me feel bad about myself so I never stepped on a scale anymore. I wasn't sure if Kebin even owned a scale.

The woman eyed me and said, "I gonna update it to a hundred and fifty-five."

I was certain I knew how she had managed to get the black eye.

"Organ donor?" she said.

"I don't really wa—"

"I'll put you down." She typed quickly. She looked up at me and said angrily, "No visible markings. You'll have to be tattooed." She handed me a laminated paper with rows of fast food chain decals, sports teams' logos, a few names of some crappy bands from twenty years ago, and some religious symbols.

"Tattooed? What if I don't want a tattoo?"

"Haveta. It's a Daxton resident requirement. All residents within the city are required ta have one visibly distinguishing mark or a limp."

"I can limp."

"I didn't see you limp when you approached the counter."

"I could start."

She shook her head at me. "Ya can't appropriate afterward. Ya have to use it to define yourself once ya become a resident." She flicked the back of the laminated paper I held with her middle finger. "Pick one."

"I don't know." My eyes raced over the options, trying to find one that best described who I was.

"Think about it during the eye exam."

She pointed at a black contraption with an attached stylus and told me to sign. I complied and she showed me the result, which was broken and choppy and looked nothing like my signature but she approved it anyway.

She hurried me down the counter and I took the eye exam. I never saw any of the blinking lights she told me to watch for because I was sure the lights weren't actually functioning and she added two restrictions to my license before ushering me toward the empty tattoo chair.

The clerk left me with a scrawny twenty-something male with a greasy and acne covered face who sniffed every five seconds. He held the dirty tattoo gun in gloveless and grimy hands and kept wiping his nose with the back of his wrist of his free hand. All his clothing appeared three sizes too big and stained as if he'd recently crawled out from under a car he was working on.

The man tilted the tattoo gun at the laminated paper still in my hand. "Whatch want?"

"None of them. Can I get an interrobang?"

"A what?"

"An interrobang. It's a punctuation mark that combines a question mark and an exclamation point."

He stared at me dumbfounded for a few seconds. "Ain't on the sheet."

"I know it's not. But I just thought—"

"Cain't do it if it ain't on the sheet." He was growing angrier. "I don't even know what that is. Probably a hipster douchebag thang."

"What if I'd already had it done before I came in?"

He shrugged. "Only a faggot would get a tattoo of sometin' like that."

"Could I go somewhere else and have it done and come back?"

"Na. Gotta be done here and now."

I examined the sheet again.

"Lady," the man said in between sniffs. "I ain't got all day. There're other people." He waved his hand to an elderly man behind me.

I handed the man the laminated sheet. "Do whatever you want."

He threw the sheet up on the counter and wheeled a table covered with little toothpaste cap sized cups over to me. The cups were filled, much of the ink spilling onto the table and mingling with dried blood. He grabbed the top of my head, leaned it to the side, dipped his gun in some black ink, and very painfully began to freehand a tattoo on the side of my neck. The process hurt like hell, seemed to take an eternity, and came to an abrupt stop. The man barked at me to move down to the photo area and ignored me when I asked for a mirror. The elderly man took my spot and the tattoo artist waved me away when I asked what he had tattooed on me.

My neck felt on fire and I stumbled to the photo area, toying with my phone and trying to remember how the reverse camera worked. I wanted to see what now permanently marked my neck.

An overweight man yelled at me to sit in the broken plastic chair in front of a blue tweed sheet and rattled off my name and address and asked me to confirm the information was correct. I told him the weight was incorrect and he scolded me for not correcting the information with the clerk and told me it was too late to change it now. He told me to stop fiddling with my phone and look at the white 'x' on the machine, which then flashed brightly and blinded me. He yelled at me to stand beside the machine and I stumbled blindly toward him. The machine belched and chirped and spit out my new driver's license.

The man grabbed my license and looked at it and then to me several times before handing it over. I blinked rapidly, still trying to clear the flash burn from my vision, and stared at my new license. I appeared confused and disgruntled and ill and there was a weeping and terribly performed tattoo of the word 'Nickelback' on my neck.

11.

Mr. Junkefeller went on an hour-long tirade about how all the services at Financial Shaming, Inc. should be priced at the amount of eighty-eight dollars because 'the Chinese' want to pay eighty-eight dollars for everything and they would think it was a great deal as long as you threw in a pair of chopsticks. He stormed back and forth in front of the cubicles shouting, "Eighty-eight dollars and a pair of chopsticks?! That's a great deal!"

Meanwhile, an overweight teen used the opossum poking stick to poke me while she laughed and told me I was old.

12.

The houses and lawns in my neighborhood were covered in black ash. As I drove toward home I noticed a dirty ice cream van parked on the road that created a T intersection catty-corner from our house. A child's jingle blared from a speaker mounted on the roof of the van. An overweight man in a soot covered soda jerk's outfit ushered a handful of gleeful and filthy children into the back of the van.

My neighbor stood at the very edge of her yard with her tiny dog and appeared as though she might topple into the street any second. The dog barked furiously at the ice cream man and children and my neighbor shifted from foot to foot, with her head cocked to the side, staring at the scene with an air of stupidity and confusion. She was covered in the raining ash and her hair appeared greasy and limp.

As I neared my driveway a small ice cream truck that might have been more of a glorified go-kart cut me off, turned the corner quickly, and slammed into the back of the parked ice cream van, narrowly avoiding hitting the other man or any of the children. A scrawny man in a mechanic's uniform hopped out of the second vehicle as a few of the children left standing outside the van quickly started to pile into the new ice cream truck. The two men began fist fighting and one of them screamed something about this neighborhood being his territory.

My neighbor still stood at the edge of her lawn as if in a trance as I pulled into the driveway. Thankfully she wasn't deterred from the commotion across the street when my car backfired. I crept along the side of the house toward the mailbox, hoping the neighbor wouldn't notice me.

The men were rolling around in the street, strangling one another, while all the children cheered. There was one lone child on the sidewalk watching the men and looking around as if she were lost. I was almost to the mailbox when the girl noticed me and the neighbor.

She possibly had blond hair. It was hard to tell from

all the grime she was covered in. She trotted across the street and approached my neighbor first. The girl left some distance between herself and the neighbor as the old woman still allowed the dog to jump and rabidly bark at the child. The neighbor directed her glazed and vacant gaze to the child.

"Hey," the girl said. "Can I live with you?"

The neighbor shifted her weight back and forth from one foot to the other rapidly but made no attempt to answer the child, only stared at her dumbly. The child repeated the question and received the same response.

The mailbox door was stuck and the metal of the box made a resounding 'thunk' when I finally pried it open. The girl and the neighbor turned to me. The neighbor surprisingly didn't seem to recognize me or break into any sort of delusional tirade. She stood and stared at me as if I were an inanimate object she couldn't quite figure out.

The child ran up to me. "Hey, lady, do you have a job?"

"Uh, yeah." I pulled a stack of random junk mail from the mailbox.

"You live here?"

"Yeah."

I tried to walk around the child and retreat to the side door before the neighbor could break herself from whatever drug induced coma she was currently in.

The girl dodged in front of me. "You live by your-self?"

"These questions are a little invasive, don't you think?"

"Can I live with you?"

"I don't think so. Your parents are probably wondering where you are. You should go home."

I tried to pass the girl again and again she blocked the sidewalk.

"My parents overdosed on heroin this morning."

"I'm sorry to hear that. But you know Daxton is the heroin overdose capital of the world, right?"

"I didn't ask for them to O.D."

"Look, kid." I placed my hand on her shoulder and gently pushed her out of my way. "Maybe you should call the police. Shouldn't you be in a home or something?"

One of the ice cream men began to slam the other's head against the side of the van. The children in the vehicles screamed with delight. A few of the children hung their soot and ice cream covered faces out the open window of the van. The neighbor stared at me and the girl as her dog barked itself hoarse. The sound space between was filled with the constant drone of Daxton and sirens and gunshots and the raging wildfire and trains and the whooping whoa whoa whoa of the numerous factories pumping whatever consumer or toxic garbage out into

Daxton.

"Please!" The girl latched on to my leg. "I don't want to go to a home! I wanna have parents who have a job and can feed me and don't beat me or spend most of their time high or living in an emotionless anti-depressant stupor!"

"Sorry, kid!" I smacked her in the face with the stack of junk mail and jerked my leg from her grasp. She stared up at me with a panicked expression. "If I wanted kids I would've had them!" I bolted for the side door.

The neighbor lady broke from whatever torpor she'd been entranced in and shouted, "Alcoholic! Can you make any more noise in the middle of the night, stupid slut!"

The neighbor's sudden outburst brought her dog, the fighting ice cream men, the child begging for a new home, and willingly abducted children in the ice cream trucks to a sudden halt. Her madness didn't faze me though as I took the opportunity to run into the house and lock the door behind me.

13.

The house was freezing. I entered the living room and found Kebin lying on the sofa wearing a parka and watching television. A large stainless steel box sat in the middle of the living room and emanated an exceptionally loud whirring sound. Hoses and cords snaked across the floor. Some of the lines ran out the window while others ran to the basement. The machine's noise permeated the house and Kebin was combating the atrocious contraption by having turned up the television's volume to full capacity. He was watching a documentary about the Holocaust.

"What is going on?!" I yelled over top of the cacophony.

"Hey!" Kebin shouted. "You're home! And you have a tattoo!"

I touched the raw skin on my neck and realized the genius of Kebin's lack of motivation for getting a driver's license. I nodded.

He squinted in the direction of my neck. "Cool! Nickelback!" He gave me two thumbs up.

"What is this?!" I pointed at the machine blasting frigid air into the living room.

"It's a morgue refrigeration unit!"

"Why?!"

"Did you know Daxton is the heroin overdose capital of the world?!"

"Yes!"

"Well, I read an article on the Daxton News website that said the city morgue is full and they're contracting out refrigeration trucks to store the bodies in until they can be processed!"

"What does that have to do with why our house feels like I'm on the North Pole?!"

"I'm going to turn the garage into a walk in freezer and rent it out to the city morgue!"

"Why is it in the living room then?!"

"I'm testing it out!"

"Couldn't you test it in the garage?!"

"The delivery guy brought it in here! I'm gonna need help getting it out to the garage!"

"I don't know if I feel comfortable with having a bunch of dead meth heads in our garage!"

The television stand rumbled with a thunderous and distorted boom as the television played a black and white image of an aerial explosion. The image cut to a line of emaciated women and children staring forlornly at whoever was filming them.

"They're not meth heads!" Kebin shouted. "They're heroin addicts! Meth went out of fashion a couple of years ago after the cold medicine crackdown! It's cheaper and easier to make heroin now! You can get prescription opiates easier than over the counter cold medication! Don't you remember the time I was peddling pseudoephedrine from other countries?!"

I shrugged and rubbed my arms. "It's so cold!"

Kebin hopped up off the sofa and began to do his dance routine. It was slower than normal as he tried to match the tempo of the mournful music from the documentary. He said, "I jump up and dance every few minutes! It keeps me from getting hypothermia! Dance with me! It will keep you warm!"

"No thanks! How about we move this thing to the garage!" I pointed at the noisy steel box.

"Okay!" He laced his fingers behind his head and be-gan to roll his hips. "How's my dancing?!"

"It's okay!"

I watched him for a few more minutes until he grew sweaty and my fingers and toes grew numb.

14.

I pulled into the parking lot of the small and weathered strip mall with three storefronts. The building and its signs looked as though they hadn't changed much since 1983 but it was hard to tell what anything actually looked like anymore since it was all covered in ash from the wildfire. If the building had been a shopping center it hadn't ever been named. The middle store was a check cashing service and I was never sure what the business on the far right was since the sign above its door didn't declare a name, only its address. The windows of the store on the far right were plastered with faded and cracked stickers advertising you could buy lottery tickets inside. I'd always thought it might've been some type of convenience store but the store itself wasn't convenient to access with a median blocking two lanes of traffic from entering the parking lot and there was a twenty-four hour gas station located right beside it. But I wasn't concerned with either of the other two businesses.

'Muricahio's Best Donuts was located on the far left and boasted "awesome", quotation marks included, on their sign with a dancing clown and the words *hot or not* which I could never put into context.

It was Sib's birthday and I was put in charge of bringing in donuts for the occasion by my other coworkers. 'Muricahio's Best Donuts was on my way to work. They didn't exactly have the best donuts but they were cheap.

I parked my car in front of the donut shop and thought I spotted a figure clad in all black and carrying an umbrella disappear around the corner of the building. I debated investigating around the building to see if it was Grim, The Unpleasant but I was already running a few minutes late and needed to get the donuts.

I entered the donut shop and was met with the stale smell of decades of cooking grease and cigarette smoke which caked the ceiling fan that didn't work and the ceiling. Several layers of dust or hair or something light gray in color and fuzzy clung to the grease. It could have been mold and I wouldn't have been surprised if it was. The entire place was much like the outside and hadn't been touched or updated since the eighties.

An old overweight man with a gin blossom nose emerged from a back room. I didn't come here often. In fact, I'd only been in the place twice before and usually a middle-aged woman waited on me. The man was wearing a yellowed and stained apron and no shirt on underneath. His arms and chest were covered in a carpet of black and gray hair. He approached the glass counter containing the donuts, leaned on it, breathed open-mouthed and stared at me expectantly.

I looked over the donuts in the display case, not knowing what to get exactly.

"I don't have all day," the man said.

"Can I get a box of mixed donuts?"

He sighed heavily and reached under the counter and slammed a box on top of the glass case. He slid the glass door for the case open with excessive force and it hit the side so hard I expected the door to shatter. But the door only stopped with a thunk and the man began to manhandle the donuts with his bare hands, slamming each one in the box hard enough that two of them bounced out and hit the floor, which pissed him off more since he had to bend over and pick them up. He smashed the floor donuts in his hairy fists before shoving them in the box and shutting it.

He dropped the box on the counter beside the register and it slid toward me.

The man punched some numbers on the register and barked, "Do you want chips with that?"

"Chip?" I said.

"Yeah, chips," he said and thumbed over his shoulder to the wire display rack mounted to the wall and filled with Junkefeller chips.

"Uh," I said, "no thanks."

He looked at me as if I'd broken wind. "We don't have anything else. You only get chips as a side."

"I don't want a side. I just want the donuts."

"The value meal comes with a side."

"Chips?"

"Yeah. Chips. Come on, lady, I don't have all day."

"I just want the donuts."

He turned abruptly from me and snapped up a bag of chips before turning back to me and throwing the chips at me. The bag hit me in the chest and fell to the floor. He pushed some more buttons and asked if I wanted the sixty-four ounce, the one hundred twenty-eight ounce, or five gallon bucket of fountain soda. I was afraid of having a gallon of soda thrown at me so I requested the sixty-four ounce before paying and making my way on to work.

15.

I drove by a neighbor on my street standing beside a motorcycle, twisting the handle and revving the engine repeatedly. On the opposite side of the street a few houses down another man stood in his front yard revving the engine of a chainsaw but there were no trees in need of pruning or cutting in sight.

Once I arrived home I found a large refrigerated truck parked in the driveway and several homeless men roaming around our front yard. I was forced to park on the street in front of the psycho neighbor's house. I wasn't too worried about a confrontation with the neighbor as she and her dog were too involved in watching and barking at Kebin as he directed two men wearing demented clown makeup and oversized jeans as they unloaded corpses from the truck and stacked them in the garage.

I exited my car and noticed the homeless men appeared to be gnawing on raw meat as they stumbled around the yard. A scraggly man wearing filthy rags had built a fort out of some old tires by the mail box and chewed on what appeared to be a human hand. One of the men blocked my path as I walked down the driveway toward Kebin and the corpse movers.

"Can I get a dollar?" the man said.

He extended his hand and dodged in front of me when I tried to pass him.

He said, "I want some coffee."

"Sorry. I don't have any cash." I added, "I'm not sure a dollar will buy you coffee anymore."

He shook his empty hand at me. "For the bus. My daughter is really sick and I need to get across town to take care of her. I just got out of prison for murder."

"Sorry. I don't carry cash."

"I'm a high-functioning alcoholic. I need money for booze. Come on, lady, liquor is all I got left."

"Sorry." I shrugged and walked past him.

"Well fuck you!" the man yelled.

I rounded the truck and Kebin noticed me.

"You're home!" Kebin shouted.

I said, "Yep."

Kebin said, "My friends Daggie and Tutu have brought us several corpses to store in the garage."

The overhead door was open and the two men dropped an overweight male corpse with a harpoon through his chest on top of a nude decapitated woman with a massive amount of red pubic hair near the far right wall. The refrigeration unit ran at full speed inside the garage. The two men shuffled out of the garage, the pant legs of their oversized jeans dragging on the concrete.

One of the men had blue triangles painted above his eyes and said, "Whadup."

The other had a green grin painted on his face from ear to ear and said, "Yo."

"Hi," I said.

"Isn't this great?" Kebin said. "They're going to pay me a hundred dollars a month."

I looked over the decaying bodies in our garage. Some of them were missing limbs and others appeared to have died by gunshot wounds. One female had an axe buried in her skull.

I said, "These don't look like drug overdoses. I thought we were storing O.D.s for the city."

Kebin said, "There's been a small change in plans."

"Hey. Yo," green grin interrupted. "You like CJG?"

His question threw me off. "What?" I said. "What is

that?"

Blue triangles said, "CJG." He plucked his T-shirt which had a picture of two men's faces screened on it with the same face paint as the corpse movers except the men on the shirt were making idiotic baby faces and the large letters 'CJG' was printed above their heads. "Crazy Jester Gang, yo. They're like the dopiest of the dope." He walked his fingers together down the length of his torso in a gesture I knew from my childhood that accompanied the song "Itsy Bitsy Spider".

"Uh, no," I said. "I haven't heard them."

"What?" green grin said. "Daggie," he slapped blue triangle's arm, "educational this old hag on the greatest duo around."

"Tutu," Kebin addressed green grin. "Can you guys unload the truck first? I want to shut the garage door and keep the bodies chilled."

Daggie pulled a cell phone from his pocket and began fiddling with it.

Tutu waved his hand dismissively at Kebin.

Kebin pointed insistently at the open door of the truck, which I noticed was still half full of mutilated corpses and one of the homeless men was now stealthily climbing into the cab of the truck. A psychotic laugh and hip-hop music distorted the small speakers of Daggie's phone. Daggie, Tutu, and Kebin instantly began to dance in a similar fashion that was part epileptic seizure and part broken robot while singing along to the lyrics boasting how homophobic the singer was. After the three of them had simultaneously shouted the word 'faggot' when the singer had sung the lyric the three formed a tight knit circle and mimed sodomizing each other while each of them said things like 'yeah, take that' and 'you want me to fuck you in the ass, faggot'.

While the three of them were lost in whatever brain-washed ignorance the song had produced Grim, The Unpleasant had appeared from around the side of the garage. Grim, The Unpleasant held his umbrella in a way I was still unable to make out his face but I was certain he was giving the trio a disapproving scowl as he watched the fake sodomy circle. After a few seconds Grim, The Unpleasant slipped into the garage and closed the overhead door without Kebin, Daggie, or Tutu noticing.

The three in front of the garage continued their impromptu frottage until the truck started. I couldn't see the neighbor or her dog with the truck blocking the way but the dog went into a series of high-pitched hysterical barks. The homeless man I witnessed earlier popped his head out of the open driver's window and screamed, "Fuck you!" before ducking back inside. A horrendous grinding noise emanated from the front of the truck before it bucked wildly. Corpses spilled out of the back of the truck and onto the driveway as it lunged forward and swerved. Daggie and Tutu yelled and ran after the truck as it barreled out of the driveway and narrowly missed my car before speeding down the street. Daggie and Tutu chased the truck.

Once the massive vehicle and the corpse movers were gone down the road there was nothing left to block the neighbor's view of Kebin and myself but she redirected her attention to the fleeing truck.

I turned to Kebin who appeared stunned by the sudden turn of events and said, "I better move my car."

As if the neighbor had supersonic hearing she slowly turned in our direction and bellowed, "Vampires! Ya'll lettin' vampires live in your shed! I'm gonna burn your house down! Call an exorcist!"

16.

I stood outside the main entrance to Financial Shaming, Inc. during my break and watched the tall flames of the wildfire in the distance. The city was now covered in six inches of ash and I turned my attention to the lump located on the sidewalk on the opposite side of the street. A couple of days ago I'd noticed an elderly woman in a velour tracksuit lying face down on the sidewalk, unmoving. Since then the ash had accumulated over her body like a forgotten piece of lawn furniture in the snow.

A rusted and beaten pickup truck I'd never seen before made its way down the dead end street toward Financial Shaming, Inc. and I wondered if Mr. Junkefeller had hired a new employee when the vehicle turned into the parking lot. The driver steered the truck halfway into the handicap spot and the crossed out section directly in front of the door which technically wasn't a parking space and killed the engine. A lanky man in a filthy T-shirt portraying a bearded and mustached man with sunglasses and a baseball cap with a car in flames above his head exited the truck. When the man approached I noted his pants appeared to be covered in black grease and his hair looked as though he had randomly cut chunks from it with scissors and used some of the grease from his jeans to style it. His face was covered in sores. Some of the sores were scabbed over and an angry shade of red skin surrounded the scabs. Other sores on his face were open and glistening with blood or infection. He stopped once he reached the door and dug an open sore on his face before addressing me.

"What's this place?" he said.

I looked at the words 'Financial Shaming, Inc.' stenciled in large white letters on the door and pointed at it. The man stared at the words for a long time, blinking slowly and digging at his face.

He turned to me after a few minutes. "What's that?"

"What do you mean?" I said.

"Whatta they do?"

"Financial shaming."

He stopped digging at his face and looked at his fingernail. He began to chew the nail and spoke around his finger. "You want some meat?"

"Meat?"

"Yeah, high quality steaks. You can't get better meat anywhere else."

"Uh. No thanks."

"Do you gotta boss or somethin'?"

"Yes."

He dropped his hand and retreated to the back of his pickup truck. His quick movements stirred up the ash on the ground and caused me to cough. He dropped the tailgate and produced a battered and grimy Styrofoam cooler. He brought the cooler back over to the door and dropped it on the ground. Another plume of ash rose up and I held my breath. He removed the lid from the cooler to reveal it was filled with ice and several unwrapped and greenish small steaks.

I said, "They look like rotten steaks to me."

The door to Financial Shaming, Inc. flew open and Mr. Junkefeller stepped out.

"What is going on here?!" Mr. Junkefeller shouted. "Who are you?! What is this?!" He kicked the cooler with his expensive pointed toe shoes and put a hole in the Styrofoam.

A couple of ice cubes tumbled into the ash on the

ground. The greasy man stared at the ice on the ground for a few seconds before turning his attention to Mr. Junkefeller.

The man said, "Ya wouldn't be interested in 2000 vintage cote de boeuf steaks, would ya? These here steaks usually retail for thirty-two hundred dollars but I only gots five of um left and I jus' wanna call it a day. I'd be willin' to let 'em go for a thousand a piece."

"Vintage cote de boeuf?!" Mr. Junkefeller said.

"Ayuh," the man said. "They yuh been aged real good ta make 'em tender and luxurious. Only the most sophisticated people eat 'em."

Mr. Junkefeller pointed a thumb at his chest. "I'm very sophisticated and wealthy! I will buy all of them!" He pulled a wallet from a hidden pocket inside of his ill-fitted blazer and counted out five thousand dollars in the form of hundred dollar bills and handed the cash to the man.

The greasy man pocketed the money and fished the greenish and unwrapped steaks from within the cooler with his grimy and bare hands. He handed the steaks to Mr. Junkefeller who shoved them into the pockets of his blazer and pants. A few maggots fell from the meat and into the ash on the ground in the process.

The man said, "I wouldn't be bothering ya to see if you're interested in a bottle of Diamond Jubilee, would I?"

Mr. Junkefeller shouted with glee, "Diamond Jubilee?!"

"Yes, sir. I gots one bottle left and would be willin' to let it go for say . . . fifty thousand dollars."

"I'll give you a hundred thousand for it! Will you take a check?!"

"Guess I could."

The man retreated to the truck and opened the passenger side door and retrieved a diamond shaped bottle with clear legs I assumed the bottle sat on. Mr. Junkefeller pulled a checkbook from a pocket inside his blazer. He scribbled on a check and ripped it from the book.

Mr. Junkefeller looked at me as he and the man exchanged the bottle and check and said, "I'm spending more money on a bottle of Johnnie Walker than you'll get paid in the next five years! How do you feel about that?! Does it make you feel worthless?! Because you are worthless! And poor!"

I said, "I don't feel anything anymore."

Mr. Junkefeller shouted, "Shut up and get back to work! Your break is over!"

17.

There were several broken and discarded children's toys covered in soot in front of the dentist's office. I entered the waiting room to find the 'children's corner' empty and the television tuned in to the Rat News Channel and the volume was maxed out and distorted. Several old people sat and nodded agreeably at the television as a man with a terrible comb over moaned openmouthed with drool hanging from his lower lip, staring vacantly off in the distance as if he was mentally defective. The banner at the bottom of the screen read 'Emperor of 'Muricahio'.

I approached the sliding glass window for the receptionist and had to shout over the groaning of the Emperor to convey my name and what time my appointment was. The receptionist wore her hair in a tight bun and was friendly but appeared nervous and wary of me. The Emperor suddenly shouted a list of racist and derogatory expletives before returning to his openmouthed groan.

An elderly woman holding a cane in the waiting room shook her fist at the television and shouted, "You tell 'em! They can get their butt fucking brown asses out of 'Muricahio if they don't like it!"

A stooped old man shouted, "They're all a bunch of criminals! Fuckin' our children and using them as slaves in their Oriental restaurants!"

Another old woman said, "I'm so glad I voted for the Supremacist Party! We need a good ethnic cleansing and genocidal rape!"

I bit my tongue and the receptionist directed me to sign my name on a paper attached to a clipboard. There were several other signatures and on one line someone had drawn a penis. I handed the clipboard back to the receptionist and was forced to sit in the waiting room for a half an hour while the Emperor delivered his monthly State of the Dissociation Address. The broadcast kept cutting in and out with the screen filling with silent static. When the static was on the television screen the elderly people slumped in their chairs as if the Emperor's appearance on the screen was what powered them. A line of wording tried to form on the screen in orange lettering but the broadcast cut back in when I tried to read it.

Eventually my name was called and I was led back to a room by a short older woman with short hair she'd colored an unnatural shade of black which made her hair look more like a wig.

I took a seat in the dentist chair and looked at the posters of kittens thumbtacked to the ceiling as the woman wheeled a table of equipment toward me and pulled on a pair of gloves. She put on a pair of glasses that magnified her black eyes and peered down at me.

"What ya here for?" she said.

When she spoke I noticed many of her teeth were missing. And the ones she still had were broken and stained an ugly brown and crooked.

"Cleaning," I said.

"Uh huh," she said.

She grabbed a scraper tool from the tray and I opened my mouth. She jammed and poked my gums with the hook end of the tool until I tasted blood and could feel it pooling in my mouth. She laid the bloody tool on the tray and picked up a tiny paper cup and handed it to me.

"Spit in this," she barked.

I complied and she sat the cup on the tray before picking up a tool I'd never seen in all my years of visiting the dentist office. They looked like pliers with a curved grasping end. I opened my mouth and she braced her free hand on my forehead before inserting the tool in my mouth. The tool closed over a back molar and the woman began to roughly jerk on the tooth. Pain shot deep into my jaw and ear. I tried to shout for her to stop but I wasn't able to articulate the words with the tool in my mouth and gave over to nonsensical shouting. I thrashed in the chair as she yelled at me to sit still. I began to punch wildly at her when my tooth popped free of my gums. The pliers hit one of my top teeth and it shattered, sending a searing pain into my skull. The woman staggered backward with the pliers, holding my bloody tooth in the tool like a prize.

Blood pooled in my mouth and I turned and began to spit it on the floor.

A woman wearing scrubs and a paper mask rushed into the room. Her eyes grew wide once she took in my state and the gleeful woman holding my extracted tooth.

"What's going on in here?" the paper-masked woman said.

A blond man in scrubs materialized in the doorway and looked at the woman holding my tooth. "Hey! What did I tell you? Get out of here!"

"I need more teeth!" the woman screeched.

The woman clasped my tooth in her hand and rushed

the two like a linebacker. She plowed in between the two of them and took off down the hallway toward the waiting room. The two people in scrubs chased after her.

The pain in my mouth was so tremendous I had trouble seeing straight. Everything was blurry and I swore I saw things in double vision. I spat more blood on the floor, knocked the tool tray over as I got out of the chair, and stumbled down the hallway toward the waiting room, holding my jaw and slobbering blood.

I didn't see anyone else in any of the other exam rooms and the receptionist wasn't behind the front desk. I entered the waiting room to the serenade of the Emperor's groaning and found a fresh round of elderly people nodding in time to some imaginary beat.

A burly man with swollen muscles and a beer belly jerked open the glass waiting room door and entered. He looked around at the old people and punched an elderly man with an oxygen tank seated by the door in the head. The old man was knocked to the floor and his oxygen tank rolled away.

The burly man shouted, "I'm establishing male dominance!" before taking the fallen man's seat.

I held my painful jaw and was forced to step over the unconscious old man on the floor before exiting the dentist's office.

18.

My jaw throbbed as I entered Jalapeño Mexican Grill. I figured soft foods would be more manageable since the broken tooth hurt like hell and for the most part Jalapeño's was all soft food as long as you didn't get their chips laden with enough salt to cause heart palpitations. Jalapeño Mexican Grill was an assembly line burrito, taco, or taco bowl fast food restaurant and was usually fairly quick when you were in a hurry on your lunch break. And it cost less than ten dollars as long as you got water to drink.

There were only a handful of people eating in. One tall, dark-haired man worked at a table behind the assembly line area with his back to the patrons. A family of four were the only ones on line to be helped. The man held a smallish male child, approximately five or six years old, on his hip. And the woman held another child with pigtails, maybe a year younger than the other child, on her hip and she kept bouncing the child periodically since the girl was squirming and sliding down her side and trying to get away. I stepped up behind them as a short, young female, barely able to see over the sneeze guard walked out of a door leading to the kitchen area. She wore a polo shirt and visor.

"Can I help you?" the girl behind the counter asked. Her name tag read 'Cribstal'.

"Yeah," the man said. "I want one burrito bowl and four burrito wraps."

"A burrito bowl and four burritos," Cribstal said, cheerfully.

She began to retrieve the items for the order but was stopped short by the man.

"No," the man said. "Did I say I wanted four burritos? I want *one* burrito bowl and *four* of the *empty* wraps. Jeez! How hard is that?"

"Four of the wraps?" Cribstal said.

The presumed wife interjected, "Did he stutter?"

"I'm sorry," Cribstal said. "I'm not sure . . . how that works." She turned to the overhead price board which contained the prices of bowls, burritos, tacos, drinks, chips, and the various salsas. "I'm not sure what the charge is for the wraps alone."

"Are you new or somethin'?" the woman with the squirming child said.

"Uh," Cribstal said. She turned to the tall, dark-haired man mixing rice at a table behind her. "Jacon, what do we charge for the wraps?"

Without turning the worker said, "It's seven ninety-five for a burrito."

"I don't want a burrito!" the male customer shouted and the child on his hip started and began whimpering.

Jacon turned around and approached Cribstal without acknowledging the family being served. The two workers conversed quietly to one another while the man and woman stared daggers at them. Jacon turned abruptly from Cribstal and went back to his station.

Cribstal said, "There'll be a dollar charge for each wrap."

"A dollar?!" the man shouted and sat the child he was holding on his feet. "I don't see you charging people who buy a burrito a dollar extra for the wrap."

Cribstal politely said, "The wrap is included in the burrito price. You asked for a bowl. Which doesn't include a wrap."

The female customer said, indignantly, "This is outrageous!"

"I'm sorry," Cribstal said. "I can get the manager if you would like to speak to them about the charge."

"I want to speak to your manager!" the female customer shouted.

Cribstal said, "Jacon. There are some people who want to speak with you."

Jacon turned and approached the counter and stared at the man.

The man waved dismissively at Jacon. "Forget it! I'll pay the four dollars for the fucking wraps!"

The child the man had sat down pulled on his pant leg. "Daddy?"

The man turned to the child and said, "Shut the fuck up before I knock your fucking head off! You whiny fucking prick!"

The child's lower lip trembled and his eyes filled with tears before he turned and buried his face in the mother's leg and began to cry.

Cribstal pulled four of the enormous wraps from a stack and carefully folded them and sat them in an empty burrito bowl before grabbing another bowl. She asked if the order was for dining in to which the man barked at her that it was. The man then proceeded to berate the girl and complain and bully her by yelling and telling her one scoop of meat wasn't sufficient to feed one person and made her dump six scoops of meat into the bowl followed by three scoops of cheese and so much sour cream the bowl was over flowing onto the counter. The man then proceeded to become irate when the girl didn't comprehend how he ordered his drink or know how to charge him. He kept repeating he wanted one extra-large drink and three small empty cups. And when Cribstal read the order's total the woman bitched about the price which was a few dollars more than the price of one meal and a deal considering they'd bamboozled the restaurant out of enough food for four meals.

When Cribstal was done with the family she made her way back down the length of the assembly area and stopped in front of me.

She smiled and said, "Can I help you?" as if she didn't just get done dealing with the most horrific people in the world.

My heart broke a little as I realized the poor girl had about two years left before it dawned on her the world was shit and people were shit and nothing was ever going to get any better and it didn't matter how nice you were to people they would always take advantage of you and treat you like garbage.

I said, "No. I don't think you can."

I turned around and left the restaurant.

19.

The wildfire was growing rapidly and it made it difficult to get home with all of the dead ends. At one point I was forced to drive through someone's yard to escape the fire as it consumed Daxton.

A few blocks from our house I drove down a road where the fire was a few feet from the sidewalk and knew it wouldn't be much longer before our neighborhood was demolished. Along the road lined with fire I spotted two men as they pulled the corpse of an emaciated woman from a pile of bodies by the bus stop. It was difficult to tell if she was emaciated when she died or if she had been dead for such a long period of time and that was the reason for the state she was in. One man held the arms of the deceased woman and the other held her legs as they swung her back and forth before launching her into the abyss of the fire.

I turned onto our road and was forced to drive partially on the sidewalk to pass a school bus parked in the middle of the road while a horde of small children clambered to get in the vehicle from the side door and the back emergency door at the same time while a straggly man with long greasy hair watched them gleefully.

People along the street were running in and out of their houses, packing their possessions into their cars. I slowed my car to watch them and overheard a woman in her pajamas berate an overweight man in sweatpants holding a box. She slapped him across the face and told him she didn't give a fuck about the family photo albums and they'd spent over seven thousand dollars on their eighty-five inch television and he better figure out how the fuck to get it in the car and she didn't care if they had to strap the children to the roof to make it happen. She then ripped the box out of the man's hands and flung it into the yard. The cardboard box cracked open on impact and several photo albums and a broken frame of what I assumed was their wedding photo spilled onto the lawn.

I thought, *I'm so glad no one ever proposed to me.*

I passed two men in their front yard. One of them

was sprawled in the grass and foaming at the mouth while the other sat beside him with a tourniquet tied around his upper arm and he injected something into his own arm.

A few houses from home a man was beating his wife relentlessly by slamming her head on the hood of a car while shouting 'whore' over and over. A small female child stood ten feet away from them, watching them serenely.

Our lawn was littered with corpses and several vagrants stumbled over the bodies, checking the pockets. One particularly filthy man gnawed on a severed human foot and stared at my car intensely as I tried to pull in our driveway but it was filled with several cars I'd never seen before.

The neighbor stood in her front yard, staring at the chaos happening in our yard. Her dog had worked itself into a frenzy. It jumped and barked and sounded as though it had barked for such an extended amount of time it had done some damage to its vocal cords. The animal pulled and lunged at the end of its leash, jerking the neighbor's arm violently, as it hoarsely barked and foamed at the mouth. The neighbor either didn't notice the state the poor creature was in or didn't care. Her main concern seemed to be the bums or the cars filling our driveway and parked in front of our house.

I was forced to pull a many point turn around and park my car in front of her house as it was the only space left. My car backfired when I killed the engine and the report drew the neighbor's attention to me.

As I exited the car the neighbor yelled, "You can't park in front of my house! I pay taxes!"

Once I stepped onto my own drive I hurled my keys at her and they made a ringing noise as they slammed into her face and dropped to the ground.

I shouted, "Move it yourself, you miserable old cunt! I'm glad you're dying alone!"

The neighbor shouted, "Oh! Oh! Oh! I'll beat your ass!" while shaking her head violently. She took a few staggering steps toward me and swung her arms as if she were wading through water which caused her to yank her dog's leash. The dog yelped in pain as she dragged it along with her.

I turned and ran up the drive and the steps, thankful the side door was unlocked. I burst through the back door and into a discord of moaning and smacking and people shouting angry and encouraging things. I slammed and locked the door behind me.

Grim, The Unpleasant stood by the kitchen sink with a glass of dark red liquid that could've been spoiled tomato juice. He still held the umbrella, even though he was inside, at such an angle I couldn't see his face. I wanted to ask what he was doing in the house but the sounds of sex permeating the house forced me toward the living room.

A naked woman lay prostrate on the floor with her hands tied behind her back and her head turned to the side while a man vigorously fucked her anus. The fucking man was facing my direction but he held the woman's ass cheeks and stared at his own cock. Three other naked men stood above the two with their backs to me, slowly stroking their cocks. A clothed man with a handheld camcorder was on his knees behind the man fucking the woman. It appeared he was focusing the camera on the man's balls and penis sliding in and out of the woman.

Daggie and Tutu sat on the sofa with a woman's disembodied torso propped up between them. Both of them fondled the breast closest to them on the torso and watched the man butt fuck the woman. Daggie had unfastened his pants and was masturbating furiously.

The television played a loop of a woman in an expensive dress holding a wine glass. The woman raised her glass in a toast and said, "Let them eat cake?" She snorted derisively. "I say let them eat their dead and save on the funeral costs." She laughed gaily and lowered the glass toward her mouth but the clip never let her take a sip before it started over again.

"Who let this old hag in here?"

I turned my attention toward the cameraman who was now standing with his camera aimed waist high at the three naked men as they continued to jerkoff in slow-motion.

The camera man glared at me and waved his hand to the side rapidly, motioning for me to move. "Get out of the shoot, lady! No one wants to see your fat old ass."

I quickly slid behind the men and rushed toward my bedroom. Kebin was blocking the doorway, back toward me. There was a new set of grunting and smacking coming from the bedroom. I stood on tiptoe to peer over Kebin's shoulder and see what was going on. My bedroom was full of men and women fucking in various positions and combinations all over my bed and dresser. The people were stacked on top of each other and some couples were fucking on top of other couples fucking.

"Hey," I said into Kebin's ear.

He started slightly and turned toward me. "Hey, you're home," he whispered.

"Why are there people fucking in my room?"

"Pile on porn," he whispered. "Isn't it great? I found this site online where you can offer up your home for a filming location and they'll pay you to use your home as a set." He pointed to the living room. "That's just light bondage." His voice raised a few octaves in excitement. "But they're letting me go last on the pile on porn." Kebin pulled off his shirt.

I noticed a man in the far corner with a camera. The cameraman said, "You're up, Kebin!"

Kebin pulled down his sweatpants to expose his erect micro penis. He stroked it with his thumb and forefinger before entering my bedroom and approaching a girl on her hands and knees on my bead, deep-throating a man with an enormous penis. Kebin slid his tiny cock in her pussy and his hips trembled in what I assumed where the biggest thrusts he could manage given how short his penis was.

I backed away from my room and decided to take refuge in Kebin's room until everyone was done. I opened Kebin's door and found a burly man holding the ankles of another man lying on his back. The burly man forced the other man's ankles up to his neck and fucked him in the ass. A blond man was bent over the bed, jerking himself off, while an old man with a beer belly kneeled behind him and sucked on the man's ball sack while finger fucking his ass with three of his fingers. A curly-haired man stood on the other side of the bed receiving oral from a boy who I would've strongly questioned if he was eighteen.

Someone hidden behind the door slammed it shut in my face. I was left standing in the small space between the living room and the bedrooms. I debated retreating to the empty upstairs but assumed I would only find more people filming pornography and honestly didn't see the point in bothering.

Suddenly the house was filled with the deafening

sound of static from the television and I cautiously crept back into the living room. The bondage fucking scene had come to a halt. Everyone was staring at the television and the orange words 'THIS IS THE LAST THING YOU'LL EVER SEE' appeared on the static-filled screen. No one moved as the screen cut to black and then to a grainy black and white scene of Brenda Lee standing in a darkened room with a single spotlight focused on her in a striped dress. An unseen band began to play her hit 'I'm Sorry' and she sang along without a microphone while bouncing slightly to the beat of the song.

The song filled the house and time and became the only thing I could hear. The song was in the floor and the walls and was coming from outside and seemed to make up the world around us.

I crossed the living room and opened the front door and was blasted with the mournful 'I'm Sorry'. A nearly blinding light filled the sky and heat radiated from the fire consuming the neighbor's house across the street and the crazy neighbor beside us ran through the flames swallowing her front yard, whirling her dog engulfed in flames above her head by its leash. I couldn't hear her or the dog or the homeless people in the front yard picking through and consuming the corpses and it was all happening in slow motion. I could only hear Brenda Lee as the flames crossed the street and driveway and began to envelop the corpses and homeless people as they ignored their fate. As if the fire were a light wind.

The flames crept closer and closer as Brenda Lee's song came to an end and the long drawn out beep of the television going off air filled the world and my head. Everything faded to white and was filled with static.

20.

This is the last thing you'll ever see.

C.V. Hunt is the author of several unpopular books.

Other **Atlatl Press** Books

Die Empty by Kirk Jones

Mud Season by Justin Grimbol

Death Metal Epic (Book Two: Goat Song Sacrifice) by Dean Swinford

Come Home, We Love You Still by Justin Grimbol

We Did Everything Wrong by C.V. Hunt

Squirm With Me by Andersen Prunty

Hard Bodies by Justin Grimbol

Arafat Mountain by Mike Kleine

Drinking Until Morning by Justin Grimbol

Thanks For Ruining My Life by C.V. Hunt

Death Metal Epic (Book One: The Inverted Katabasis) by Dean Swinford

Fill the Grand Canyon and Live Forever by Andersen Prunty

Mastodon Farm by Mike Kleine

Fuckness by Andersen Prunty

Losing the Light by Brian Cartwright

They Had Goat Heads by D. Harlan Wilson

The Beard by Andersen Prunty

www.ingramcontent.com/pod-product-compliance
Lightning Source LLC
Chambersburg PA
CBHW011508170626
46812CB00009B/3028